Courageous Convictions

COURAGEOUS CONVICTIONS

First edition. June 21, 2020.

Copyright © 2020 Angie Kesler.

Written by Angie Kesler.

Cover illustration by Patrick Kesler.

This book is dedicated to: my dad, who encouraged me to put my feelings down on paper at a very young age, my husband, who respects my time to do so and pushes me to always be my best, and my best friend, Meaghan, who pumps me full of encouragement each and every day!

ALL THAT REMAINS

We talk, we talk in circles.
Repetition doesn't fix broken.

We walk, we walk the same path.
But the steps lead nowhere.

We love, we love whole-heartedly.
Yet the heart remains scarred.

We bleed, we bleed for truth,
Trusting in the unknown.

We hope, we hope for a new beginning,
Because hope is all that remains.

EMPATHY

You don't need to stand on the mountaintop
To understand the awe of the valley

You don't have to hang from tree branches
To star gaze

You don't have to dig a grave
To know the pain of losing someone

You don't have to play an instrument
To feel the passion of the music

   Just as...

You don't have to walk a mile in someone
else's shoes
To know we all bleed the same

You just have to love them with all of your
heart.

IT MATTERS

Sometimes it matters
-that look on your face
Sometimes it matters
-that empty space
Sometimes it matters
-those words that seep out
Sometimes it matters
-those thoughts of pure doubt
      LINGERING
In the shadows
      IMPINGING
Life´s particles
      LEAVING
Pieces of me
      BEHIND

STUCK

He consumed me whole
Then spit me out
Piece by piece

But not completely

He retained just a few small,
But crucial pieces
Of my heart

Just enough to keep me
From giving myself
Fully to another

Just enough to know
I could not move
On without him

Then he gnawed on them
From time to time
Keeping our hearts
Intertwined

And I let him-
Because even though it hurt,
It kept him a little bit closer.

STARTING OVER

Putting my heart on the line,
And my faith in God
Taking one breath at a time
Releasing negative thoughts from my mind.

Igniting the passion
Consuming all doubts,
Knowing risks must be taken
Somewhere, somehow.

Keeping honesty foremost
Excluding lies from all words
Sacrificing each moment,
While leaning into the curves.

Exploring the body
And all it entails
Reaffirming hope
That new life prevails.

TODAY I MADE IT

Today I made it
I am right where I am supposed to be-in this
moment-my destiny

Today I made it
I climbed another rung when I was called-I
did not heed-I did not stall

Today I made it
Over the mountain set before me-I may have
tired-yet he let me see

Today I made it
I conquered emotion I thought improbable-I
needed coaxing-I opened the Bible

Today I made it
He sent strength in human form-I leaned on a
shoulder-I avoided more harm.

I made it!

WHO I AM

I talk
I talk too much
It's in my DNA
What else can I say?

I think
I think things through
Hash it out in my mind
And give it time.

I feel
I feel deeply
Heart on my sleeve
Try my best to believe

I laugh
I laugh often
Cause life is short
So please don't distort...
Who I Am

COLLAPSE

To get up again and again
After the waves come
To listen to the hounds howl
And know it can stop soon
Like a collapsible paper doll
Easy to hold, but easier to crumble
Firmly held by the wrong reigns
Some weeks I remember
how hard it is to breathe
I will not watch you collapse
Like I did.

BACK BURNER

On the back burner
Left to simmer
My love for you steadily growing thinner

Phone calls and a text
To say good night
You think that effort will hold me tight?

Not for long, this girl is slipping
Out of your grasp
Wonder if you'll miss me?

Odds were always stacked against us
I fought for you
Then you destroyed my trust

I'm moving on cause life feels empty
What I thought we had
Faded so quickly.

EMPTINESS

The troubled soul has
  Time to fill

It knows not where nor
  When to be still

It aimlessly wanders
  In agony

It squanders away life´s
  Simplicities

Hour by hour,
  Day by day

As light fades to darkness
  And sadness to shame

These simple actions
  The soul lacks to observe

For its neglect of attention
  Has lost all preserve.

YET I LINGER

The Silence
Deafening
The Emotions
Confusing
The Intentions
Concealing
The Ramifications
Threatening
Yet I Linger...

FAITH

Peaceful pleasures settle in the depths of the
soul,
And the memories created are treasures.

Emotions take hold of the genuine heart,
Creating storms of clarity for believers.

Leaving strength to rebuild what's been
shattered.
Forsaking none of the deaf or the blind.

Restoring faith in the lost of yesterday.
Calling all to heed no longer.

For the innocence lost,
Is not to despair.

And the realization of its gravity
Weighs heavy on the mind.

Yet new life is your reward,
For the higher power is truly divine

So be cautious with your words
Do not spew untruths freely

Because the forces above are greater than all

And you need not doubt your own identity.

DOUBT

WALLS-we break them down, but

DOORS-keep slamming shut, and

FEARS-are building up cause

LIFE-can be too much to swallow.

CHOKE-on the words we speak, but

LOVE-can make us complete;

TRUST-to make it work, yet

DOUBT-consumes you.

DISCOVERY

Found a canvas stretched as far as you are
That paints what you want others to see

Mixed the colors to blend a new meaning
Since your beauty was only skin deep

Used stain blocker to hide imperfections
Picture framed your face out with some gold

Now there's no need to reveal your true
colors
Cause your conscience has already been sold.

CHOICES

Find solace in the rhythms
That move you.

Take hold of the passions
So real.

Release the negativity
That binds you.

Expel the decisions
That cause you strife.

One life.
Your choices.

IGNITE

Cover me, protect me from the storm.
The lightning and thunder will do me no
harm.
The pain of the downpour, the hail, and the
floods
Cannot draw me away from your comforting
touch.

The sparks of the fire
The ashes that float
As the embers crackle and ignite the mind
and heart
Will never, ever keep us apart.

MAKES ONE FORGET

Less emotion does not
Equate to less pain
Though it may seem

Silence does not mean
Peace lives within
Though it may deceive

The passing time, now lost.
Waiting...why?
Investments always supersede
The rising costs.

Walking away does not
End the struggle
Though lost time
Makes one forget.

IT FAILS

Eyes focus differently
We know this, and yet
We struggle to
Understand why we don't
See eye to eye.

Minds are unique
And regardless of
Individual thoughts
We are tormented
By others decisions.

Hearts beat separately
Still we long
To become one
And are destroyed when
It fails.

DECEIVED

I look in the mirror
I see an aging face
The wrinkles that formed
From this long, hard race.

Worry from within
Seeping out my pores
That masks the me I used to be
Before the heartbreak wars.

The essence of my being
That eludes to fulfillment
Is a mind trick to onlookers
Not a true life of endearment.

So take me as I am
But please do not be fooled
Cause these wrinkles on my aging face
Show my fight in this cruel world.

RUN

When you want to run
Where do you go?
Hiding in the shadows,
Feeling empty and alone.
Escape to the safety,
Where comfort can be found.
Where he understands you
Without you making a sound.

Where you can be you
And he listens cause he knows.
Where there's always refuge
And love and laughter grows.
Is this where you were meant to be?
How long will it take for you to see?

Why do you live this life of doubt?
Blowing in the wind, heart jumbled about.
When the security and passion
is close enough to touch.
When the one who made your world turn
Cares so much...and you run.

FROM THE ASHES

I don't know if you know who you are, til you
lose who you are.
It's then that you discover who you want to
be.
It's then that you see what life should be.

I don't know if you know how it hurts, til you
hurt the one you love.
It's then that you feel deeper than you
thought possible.
It's then that you can't catch your breath.

I don't know if you know how to stand, til you
stand alone.
It's then that you find strength within.
It's then all you have is your own willpower.

I don't know if you know how God loves, til
you hit rock bottom.
It's then that his light is finally seen.
It's then that you truly believe.

FORGIVE YOURSELF

For giving away your power to those that
abuse it
For not knowing better at the time
For past behaviors
For your survival patterns
For being whom you needed to be, instead of
who you wanted to be
For wanting to see the best in people who
always fail you
For letting others break you
For loving people who don't respect you and
love as you deserve
For saying things you didn't mean
For believing distorted truths
For negotiating your morals
For staying in the wrong place for just a little
too long
For dividing your time among the unworthy
For the apprehension you feel with new
relationships
For not listening to your better judgment
For being human

But Never Forget.

IDEAS

Bundles of pain
Leave ugly stains

Indigo skies
As she cries

Brush it under the rug
I've never seen love

Take anything you want
Just leave my heart

Resurrecting memories
That destroy myself

LOSING MYSELF

I do believe I'm losing myself again,
deep in thoughts that kill me.

Twist my heart and tangle my soul,
mangle my mind til I lose all control

Cause I don't understand
People at all.

The lack of commitment,
The need for themselves

To leave others behind
Without any care.

So I turn to my pen
To find some answers.

I write and I bleed,
Yet I find deceit

That swallows and
Consumes me.

When actions don't match words,
Do words hold any truth?

When words lose their meaning,
Is there even any use

In pushing forward and trying so hard
To build a relationship with so many scars?

Cause the person you are
And you long to be

Is not the person
That belongs next to me.

I don't know how to tell you,
You make me feel used.

I'm seeing the true you,
And it's leaving me bruised.

My heart crumbles thinking
You'd do this again.

But even more hurtful,
That you tried to begin

To put on that front
Act as if you still care,

Cause the man you promised
Is far from there.

Beyond repair
Life is not fair
Yet I dare
To trust
And
Lose.

THINKING

Fresh ideas of what is to come
Lingering in the breeze
Revolving around the clouds
Disintegrating into newness
Bringing hope to the weary
Inspiration to the artists of the unknown
Hours passing, bringing moments
  Of uncertainty.

HOLD ON

Hold on to what makes you smile
Even if it's ridiculously silly

Hold on to what you believe in
Even if you stand alone

Hold on to what you must do
Even if it's a long way from where you
thought was home

Hold on to yourself
Even if it seems easier to let it all go

Hold on to my hand
Even when I've gone away.

NOTES

I spread myself so thin
I may blow away in the wind
I feel deeper than most
Give my time away to those
Who don't even know
Or understand me
I cry, worry, shake, and laugh
Til they break me

Void
Hollow
Empty
Blank
Vacant
Nugatory
Null
Invalid

My crushed spirit is a result
Of the judgements
They invoke.

NOT SO WISE

Mom used to say, just curb that tongue,
Don't say anything at all...

So why is it that I'm speaking;
spewing, spitting negativity into my own
head?

How do you tug, pull, rip, shred me to pieces
Then look at me wondering why I feel
shattered?

And if my life is my own,
Why do so many try to control it?

Mom used to say, just curb that tongue,
Don't say anything at all...

But she never told me
Don't think it!

HOMES THE SOUL

What moves you?
Really jolts your heart, mind, soul?

Is it music?
Compelling conversation?
Nature at its finest?

What inspires and drives you?
Really wakes your heart?
Shakes your soul
Breaks your silence?

Is it purpose?
Divine grace?
Lust for something greater?

What homes the soul?
Really makes you...
Really soothes you...
Really exposes your beauty...

YOUR REFLECTION

REACH

When I need a moment
Without struggle
When I see the waves
Come crashing in
And the surges of electricity
Take me over
I am shocked into
My own reality

That to be with you
Is to be alone
And I choose it
Again and again
Letting the pain
and solitude back in

When I reach for that
Warm embrace
But you're not even
Close enough to make a sound
Nowhere to be found
And I know it
But still I reach
Into the emptiness

And am shocked into
My own reality

That to be with you
Is to be alone
And I choose it
Again and again
Thinking I may win
You over.

POWERLESS

What can I say when it falls on deaf ears?
What can I do when I'm powerless?
When the circumstances are out of my hands,
Yet the situation destroys us both in different
ways?
When I believe with all that I am that actions
speak louder than words
-And you are stagnant-
Watching, waiting as the minutes turn to
hours and months to years.
When I cry for your loss, but you push
through, empty yet knowing
When I know I am blessed, and can
appreciate all I have
-while you stand solemn-
And incomplete, incapable of loving the way
God intended.
I may be defeated, but you're lost,
Travelling a passionless trail to
solitude...Move, Feel, Attack, It's Time!

JANUARY

Peculiar
It may seem
Peculiar
Indeed

To proceed
As we choose
As though
There's nothing
To lose.

Ravenous
It appears
Ravenous
Doubtlessly

To risk
It all
As we do
As though
There's something
To prove

Lunacy

PAYOFF

The hunger
Longing
Avidity
Itch

The urge
Salacity
Thirst
Craving

The desire
Sensuality
Lechery
Appetite

The hazard
Peril
Jeopardy
Plunge

The speculation
Contingency
Fortuity
Possibility

The payoff
¨Us¨

STALL

She sits
Hidden
Away

Wondering
Should she
Stay

Will anyone notice?
Will anyone care?

She sits
Tucked
Within

Assuming
Her thoughts
Will win

Does she know?
Can she see?

She sits
Hidden
Away

CRUSH

Night of lust
Broken sink
Regrets it later
Overthink

One more message
Meet again
Pull me in
Know it´s a sin.

CLICK

With the click of a button
Your life can change
You never know for certain
What tomorrow will bring

So enjoy each moment
Savor each experience
Smile through the troubles
Always remain curious

In the end you´ll see what matters
Positive vibes will remain
When the right one comes along
Nothing needs to be explained

EXISTENCE IS FUTILE

Welcoming rock bottom again
If you dig long enough
You´ll always find more dirt-
More hurt,
So I don't dig.

Yet it finds me, binds me
Instead of letting me go,
It intertwines me
In your web of lies, criticize
And demean me
You think you can scheme me?

Incarcerate me, penetrate me-
Rape me over and over
The scars will remain
Life does not change
My value diminishes each minute.
No matter how you spin it.

Your secrets destroy me
Thrown in my face to tear at my soul
You like to watch me lose all control.
You win, I lose,
In the end - what´s the use?
Scars were multiplied, not removed.

OVERRATED

Your smile is outdated
Faded
Overrated
Cause when you said you'd catch me
If I ever fall
You were nowhere to be seen
Your words cut like knives
Your eyes pierce my heart
You look like Romeo
But you do not play the part
So go where you may
And lie where you desire
My soul turned
From loyalty
To stone.

SHATTERED

Don't lie, it's not worth it
Don't lie, walk away
If you hide what you´re doing
You know it's not okay.

You shattered your character
I let you rebuild it
Don't need you, don't want you
Walk away, don't destroy me.

You knew it would kill me
You knew that I cared
You did it anyway,
No feelings to spare.

If that's how you live
I don't want any part
If that's how you live
You don't deserve my heart.

DON'T BLINK

Tiny wings perched
Upon a branch
Often takes more than
Just one glance
To appreciate the beauty
We all should share
To acknowledge it's finest
With intricate care
For when taken for granted
We see but a bird
We overlook nature's
Most important features
We are blind to the necessity
Of God's unique creatures
For those wings will soon fly
And that moment
Has passed us by.

DO YOU?

When hearing truths
You've yearned to know
When worrisome thoughts
Inside you grow
Do you value honesty?
Do you retreat to safety?
Do you guard your heart?
Do you act too hastily?
When your heart finally opens
And lets someone in
When you start from scratch
And begin once again
Do you trust new beginnings?
Do you hope for a sign?
Do you secretly wonder?
Do you cherish the time?
When smiles supersede tears
And your heart beats with passion
When you realize that God
Provides you love everlasting
Do you drop to your knees?
Do you renew your faith?
Do you open the good book
And believe what it says?

FALLING APART

Rejection is a hard thing to swallow
Until you experience the pain, you can't see
Rejection takes over the heart, soul, and mind
Leaves you scarred, bent, and broken like me.

Now you want me to forget, and move past it
But the visions so clear in my mind
Of the history of love that I wasted
While you so easily left me behind.

You knew all along what was happening
As you led my happy heart into darkness
I wore blinders without even caring
Cause all I tried to do was for us.

But now I want this to work
And it's failing, it's clear
With blinders removed
I'm still gasping for air.

I don't know how to ease the fears that I feel
I don't know how to escape the thoughts
I don't know how to break without breaking
us
Where's your hand as I'm falling apart?

BIO

You wish you could trust
Like you used to before the lies.
And you dream of the way you used to be.
You are feeling a void.
You used to know your worth,
But now you question everything.
You seem to be hollow,
But you´re really just lost.

NO RESOLVE

Moments filled with unimportant chatter
Knowing that none of it really even matters
Standing to the side, staring at me

Oblivious to the claws still reaching for me
Attention needed, but I cannot oblige
Cause I am just tissue, with nothing inside

Desires at the forefront, no matter the cost
It's over, I am spent, finished
I'm done-no resolve to show
Only time left to pack up and go.

BETTER

I've always believed that I don't let other
people change who I am and want to be.
Tonight I realize that notion is untrue. The
fact is, they cause a drastic change in me.
People's actions cause me to guard myself
and question my own thoughts
-But mostly-
They challenge me to look at myself
differently. They influence me in a positive
way-where I want to be a better version of
me-so as not to do things that are
questionable, but more honorable.
The me that I have come to see is not faulted,
but pushed to be better.

OTHERS

Sometimes we have to help others
When we can no longer help ourselves

Everyone needs an angel
Everyone needs a hero
Everyone needs a friend

Sometimes I look at him and think
Is he ever going to be free
From the demons in his head
The hauntings of yesterday

Scars make you beautiful
Oh, so beautiful
Don't fade away.

CHANCES

Lost my balance

Between your wrongs and lies

Stumbled over the words

Two too many times

Tripped on reality

Let you back in

Picked up the pieces

Started all over again.

FOR REAL?

Did I love you too deeply?
Did I hold you too close?
Was my honesty too bold?
Was my heart too cold-
   To grasp it tight?
Was letting it go easier?
Was that your answer?
Was walking away better?
Were you thinking,
   ¨Wish I wouldn't have met her.¨?
Cause it tore me apart.
Left holes in my heart
   You cannot repair...
Left me trapped there.

YOU

When I lay down at night
Your arms nestled around me;
My spine curving up into your chest,
That's when I´m me.

You´re the perfect tune
That lulls me to sleep.
You breathe so heavily,
The heat from your body warms me.

I feel truly secure for the first time.

There's a sensation I get
When we're intertwined
That makes me realize what I have.
Your eyes brighten the room, keep you on my mind.

I won't take you for granted.
I´ll tend the seed we've planted.
I´ll have your back, walk beside you
When you're feeling lost, I´ll guide You.

FAILING

Life throws you curves,
and it's easy to see,
what's good for you
isn´t right for me.

What you want
is not what I need.
Love isn't going to
conquer anything.

SHADY

Shady people playing games
Only have themselves to blame.
When reality bites back
Be ready for the attack.

Don´t mess with me
Cause you will see,
It's yourself you are jerking
       around.

ME?

I thought you had changed;
That your words were true.
I thought that you missed me
Like I missed you.

You vowed it would be different,
To put me first
You promised no lies,
but delivered hurt.

Yes, then it happened.
You broke your word again.
You jumped back in the ring
Like you forgot what you´d said.

So now I´m left wondering
Did I make a mistake?
Is my heart in your hands
Only to allow you to break
            Me?

DOESN'T MATTER

Throw caution to the wind, and you throw
your heart out the door.
Your lesson is not learned and you know it.

Confide in a human and you will be
disappointed.
Man will fall and fault you over and over.

Doesn't matter how upstanding you are.
Doesn't matter how loyal.

Doesn't matter that you always had his back.
It's the nature of the beast.

Put your heart out there, it will be shattered.
Put your faith in someone, it will be
destroyed.

Say I love you,
and it is over.

RAINBOWS AND BUTTERFLIES

Rainbows and butterflies
What the happy people see.
Rainbows and butterflies
Avoiding this world of misery.

Lilacs and daffodils
What the hopeful people see.
Lilacs and daffodils
Blooming for you and me.

Dragons and unicorns
What the mysterious people see.
Dragons and unicorns
Soaring above the land and sea.

Selfless sacrifice and giving trees
What the thoughtful people see.
Selfless sacrifice and giving trees
Pouring out of hearts and leaves.

Yellow lights and red flags
What the cautious people see.
Yellow lights and red flags
Flashing and waving for eternity.

Smiles and unending laughter
What the funny people see.
Smiles and unending laughter
Resonating through the breeze.

Featherbeds and eyes of red
What the tired people see.
Featherbeds and eye of red
Screaming for some peace.

Lightning crashes and thunder
What the broken people see
Lightning crashes and thunder
Destroying harmony.

TIME

A calming silence surrounds
Yet minds work overtime
The peaceful bubble of soothing waters
Fills silence with thoughts sublime
Radiating smiles consume
Force chills to further days
Time creeps in so slowly
But quickly washes away
The notion of life everlasting
Too soon has come to pass
For the darkened hours of moonlight
Are overcome with sunshine at last.

EMOTIONALLY SCARRED

No fault of yours
Needing more
No fault of your
Emptiness linger
No fault of yours
Loneliness consumes
No fault of yours
She's broken
No fault of yours
Wanting you
All your fault!

JUST MEMORIES

A cup of coffee
A four leaf clover
A cigarette
A cross
A tear stained pillow
Reminders
Life´s journey-
Just passing through
Gone

AFFLICTED

An afflicted heart from the start
I tried to amend your soul
You were a broken spirit
But I couldn't hear it.
You hid it well
An afflicted soul
Spinning out of control
Nowhere to go.

FATALITY

You said you loved me
I risked it all
You said you loved me
Then watched me fall
I bruised myself
Among the pile of bones
Wasted my time putting you
Up on that throne.
Cause you didn't deserve it
It's all rather unnerving.
Do you call that love?
Cause your heart was swerving
Another direction
You had no connection
And you purposefully deceived me
Kept saying that you needed me
But in the end : reality
Your love was a fatality.

YOU, SIR...

You, sir...
Can find commonalities
With anyone.
Don't mistake intriguing
Conversation
For love.

NEEDS

A nervous embrace
Warm lips touch her face
Arms wrapped tight
This anticipated night
He spoke all the right words
Knew all her needs
She wanted him more
Than he could conceive.

BOOK OF LIFE

It's easy in this life to be drug down
Negativity lingers, dishonesty brews
Friendship becomes a word so misconstrued.
They say fools rush in, so here we are
Trying to forget former battle scars.
Sometimes I think I know you
Then I realize I'm wrong
I'm struggling to know just where I truly
belong.
Every time I start to believe this is what is
meant to be
Something seems to happen that brings me to
my knees.
You know I'm here waiting, but we seem to be
fading
This life I´ve been leading has become
frustrating.
Nothing is left but pain, I'm struggling to get
by
I need something from you that´s continually
denied.
I have spoken, trust was broken, forced to
end another chapter.

LET GO

Standing on the ledge
Enough has been said
Praying for a sign
Is it all a waste of time?

Thoughts racing through my mind
Heart pounding overtime
Is this what I want to do?
Are my thoughts misconstrued?

Taking a step back
Clearer thinking intact
His message now clear
I am still needed here.

EDGE OF EXILE

Blue flames
Cool waters
The sun won't fall the way
You used to for me

Hard ground
Slow hours
Evening hushes in through
Dead leaves

While reasons winter over

Stifled teardrops
Burning questions
My mind wanders
Aimlessly for truth

The Edge of Exile

BLAME GAME

Cheaters don't change
Liars rearrange
The truth
For their use...
Peace of mind
Then they rob you blind
Act like it's your fault.

LET YOU GO

You were my strength when I had none
And when you walked away, I let you go.

Not because I wanted to, but because I knew
It was the right thing for you.

People tell me things
Happen for a reason

It may not seem like it,
But I have not abandoned you, ever

When you text or call, I´m here
Always have been...

So be upset, hate me, whatever suits your
needs.
But remember, I never completely left you.

HEART OF STONE

Why do we do the things we do?
The choices we make are binding.
The judgments we make, often wrong.
Cold, callous heart of stone.

BEING ME

My mind is tired of thinking
I´m tired of running
Hiding from reality
Peeking through the trees
Hoping it doesn't see me
Escaping seems easy
Easier than being me.

HERE

Don't just hear me, listen.
Don't just respond, think.
It's not always what you say,
Sometimes it's how you say it.

My forgiveness is not my weakness.
My loyalty is not a front.
My need for understanding,
May have made you want to run.

So I'm still here and questioning,
5 months down the line.
Will we make it? Are you faking?
Is it all a waste of time?

FEAR

Fear can devour you, rule you
It makes you who you are
Instead of who you want to be
Intensifies your reality

Fear can drive you, propel you
It makes you do things
Out of character
Pushes you to the brink

DON'T LOOK

Sneaking suspicions
Lurking behind you
Like shadows in the night

Constantly on guard
You walk faster
As they will you to let them back in

SELF

My worst self
Generational curses
Thrust into a life I did not choose
Crumpled pillows, filthy sheets
Sucking me dry
I no longer feel myself

SALVATION

Spitting these scriptures like bullets
Can't take my faith, I rule it
Raised in the church, knowing God
You've got no religion, that's odd
Find your savior!

JUST WORDS

¨I love you¨ were just words to you.
But for the first time in my life, they meant
something to me.
And I couldn't blame you.
Because I had said it before and didn't mean
it at all.
I mean, I thought I did, til I met you.
And I realized how badly you could hurt me,
Like no one else ever could.
My heart unguarded was dangerous in your
presence
Because your feelings were vacuous.
And no matter what I said or did, your selfish
soul was beyond my reach.
So I watched...
I watched you turn, put those shades on, and
mount that Silverado, poised as ever.
I watched you turn that key, never once
glancing back;
As the tears streamed down my nose
And dribbled off my lip, into my lap.
I watched...
I watched you drive away as I gasped for air
Knowing that I was the broken piece of your
puzzle,
Yet wishing I was the missing one.

WHO CARES

I am plagued with emotionless emotions.
So many walls built up, so many stories
untrue
That the numbness that surrounds me
Makes me feel absolutely nothing for you.

I want to feel anger, pain, or despair
But the sea of emotion leaves nothing there.
No grief, no sorrow, no joy, no smiles,
Just outstretched arms of nothing for the
while.

I try to escape, yet there's nowhere to go,
But into the emptiness of my own soul.
An endless, blank body of emotion it spares,
Cause in the end I can´t be the one who cares.

GRASPED AND DANGLED

You slid your way back in,

Knowing the scars you left.

You tangled the strings of my heart.

You grasped me from behind.

Knowing the pain remained,

You dangled the pieces I longed for.

You turned the tables swiftly,

Knowing the price I´d pay when

You strangled me and walked away again.

DISAPPOINTMENTS

The disappointments
The disregard
The selfish choices made

She's losing it
The passion
The longing
The lust for love and life

The paths they take
Are broken
Separated, split
Haphazard

She questions her decisions
Nothing is as it seems
The road is desolate
Her heart-drained
Strained

Regaining her composure
Has become a struggle
She desires more
She sacrifices everything
She gives up

SOCIAL MEDIA DESTRUCTION

I'm talking - you´re elsewhere
I´m loving - you scroll
                        You click
                                You message
                                        You flirt
I don´t

I don´t understand how to deal
I don´t understand what you feel

I don´t

You ¨wave¨
You send videos
You reminisce
You snap selfies - send them
          But not to me

I don´t

So I don´t understand your ways
I don´t want to gaze into your vacant eyes any
longer.

WRITER'S AFFIRMATION

I am doubtful
I value honesty
I write to clear my head
I trust no one
I honor loyalty, and my pen
I give voice to truth
I give voice to reason
I am transparent
I make the days count
I hold onto those I love
I am dedicated
I make life matter

TWO YEARS AGO YESTERDAY

Two years ago yesterday
You said you'd have my back

Two years ago yesterday
I had hope we wouldn't collapse

Two years ago yesterday
I had faith in what we were

Two years ago yesterday
I gave you my honest word

Two years ago yesterday
We had only just begun

But two years ago yesterday
I was convinced I'd found ¨the one¨.

Seven months later
I had to accept the reality

Seven months later
You said that we weren't meant to be

Seven months later

I tried to erase you from my heart

Seven months later
I was forced to make a fresh start

Seven months later
I mended what was left

Seven months later
I replaced you, and that was it

But seven come eleven
I knew a piece was missing

Seven come eleven
And I couldn't keep on guessing

Seven come eleven
I tried to keep my distance

Seven come eleven
I could not continue the resistance

Seven come eleven
And I let you back in

Seven come eleven

INTERNET CHAOS

Personal Connections
Lost love redirections
Constant imperfections
Lovers' misconceptions
Flirty destructions
Persistent disruptions
Closed door corruption
Vacant assumptions
Violent reactions
Temporary satisfaction
Diminishing attraction
Evaporation adaption
Appalling abduction
Meaningless seduction
Unmoving deduction
Loyalty assassin

NARCISSIST

It's not about you this time, but twist it so it
is.
Excessive thoughts of your value motivate
you to live.
Admire yourself and spread it thick cause
others won´t see through you
Push the blame on someone else cause you
already know it's not true.

It can´t be you who makes mistakes, that is
plain to see.
So place that guilt elsewhere, but this time it
won't be on me.
It's not about you this time, but twist it so it
is.

PHOTOGRAPH

Silence is my first language

My mind is a darkroom

Agitating my scattered thoughts

Developing the negatives

Everything is black and white

Rinsing the slate clean,

Hanging them up to dry

Total exposure.

BLEED

Always left ¨e¨motionless
I bleed poems
All over the pages
Seeking serenity
An outlet for my fears
Finding solace in my pen
To organize my thoughts
Expel them from my mind
To settle my worry.

OUCH

Yesterday shoved me.
      I started counting my troubles
            cause time was running short.
      I started reevaluating my priorities
            cause regrets were not an
option.
      I started analyzing problems
            cause I wanted to tackle
solutions.
      I started appreciating what I have
            cause too soon it can all
vanish.

GOSSIP

Did you know,
Have you heard
She said what?
Oh my word...
The gossip queen is back in town. Watch what
you say when she's around.
Angie is pregnant,
Maria quit.
Wait, that isn't accurate.
Meaghan's out,
Wonder where she is.
Did she really call in sick?

Doesn't really matter,
I'll go tell Terry.
Then head to tell Cathy
In the library.
All this news,
Doesn't matter if it's true,
Just got to be a part
Of the gossip crew!

Mike's gone again
I think Phil's hungover.
Julie's with Will
It's a hostile takeover.

Is it time for her to retire?
Hell no, what would she do?
She wouldn't have the info
To always misconstrue!

ENTITLED

For every action there is a reaction.

You don't like my reaction to your action, well screw you, then.

I´m entitled to my feelings about how you treat me.

I´m entitled to the life I want.

I'm entitled to say what I need to say.

Doesn't mean it is going to fix anything between us, but at least you can´t say you didn't know where I stood on the situation.

So rage about it, or ignore it...either way, it was aired. No regrets.

ODE TO DAD

He is a hammer and a screwdriver
He is goofy faces and an arm punch
He is funding the down payment of our new
house in a credit crunch

He is Rocky Road ice cream and Reese's
Peanut Butter cups
He is encouraging and loving advice when I
need a pick-me-up

He is grandpa to my children and dad to my
brothers and me
He is a beach chair and a fiction book
He is the teacher of how to bait my hook

He is a Landshark or bourbon and a Grand
Marquis LS
He is a leaf blower and a wood stacker
He is a helpful pro/con list

He is puller of the inner tube behind the black
jet ski
He is a can of golden oak stain and a chore list
before I leave
He is the purchaser of the outfit that looks
like a bumblebee!

SERENITY

Darkness cloaks the sky
As the sun slowly fades
Her mind wanders

Fireflies light up the night
As the coyotes wail
Her heart stifles

Breezes ruffle the leaves
As limbs crackle
Her soul settles

Serenity

NEWNESS

Sifting through the memories
Her pipe dreams turned to ashes;
Blew away into the ocean
Steering her on a new course
Away from the familiar

The horizon before her
A never-ending splash
Of breathtaking unknown colors
Echoing her name faintly;
Summoning her into the evening light

Issues at hand
fade into nothingness
She no longer questions
But follows whole heartedly
Never to look back

ODE TO MOM

She is vanilla candles and folded towels
She is smiles and a listening ear
She is a ride on the deck boat with wind
blowing through our hair

She is baked goods, yet salads and cheese and
veggie trays
She is Mich Ultra and Miller Lite
when it's time to play

She is grandma to my children and mom to
my brothers and me
She is a good book and toes in the sand
She is a cup of black coffee in hand

She is patience at its finest
She is a cold glass of iced tea
She is kept promises, soft spoken words, and
the queen bee.

UNBREAKABLE

Strength takes over, but I'm not unbreakable.

Hardships harbor, but they're not unbearable.

Truths are told, but it's undeniable.

Lies spring forth, but they're unforgivable.

God can heal, and it's irrefutable.

Prayers bring peace, and it's indisputable.

NOT

Landscapes, not portraits
Show true beauty
Capture the scenery
Embrace the memories
Leave lasting impressions

Tapping, not beating
Resonates sound
Echoes the music
Penetrates the soul

Whispers, not screams
Gain attention
Deliver the message
Calm the masses

IT SEEMS

I've never met your standards
Probably never will
But there's a man
Who doesn't judge
And knows that life's not fair.

Who picks me up
When I get down
Who lets me know he cares.
Who understands me
Inside out
And has my cross to bear.

He carried it
For you and I
And though you cannot see
We will always meet his standards
When we are on our knees.

SPEAK

Can't remember?
Don't recall.
Did you tell me?
Nothing at all.

When I speak,
You just don't listen.
Distracted by whatever
You choose valuable instead.

You hear me, you nod.
You acknowledge I'm speaking.
You respond with a phrase
That has no actual meaning.

No relation to the topic
I'm trying to relay;
Because when I speak
You go miles away.

SWITCHING GEARS

There's no real respect, brush me to the side
Can't tell me the truth, always something to
hide

Take me for granted, make assumptions I'll
stay
Why should I try, when I'm just in the way

Next time that I'm needed, I'm switching
gears
Reach for my hand, and there's nobody here

To solve all the problems, and keep it
together
Resolve the issues, no matter the weather

Keep pushing me out, 'stead of pulling me in
Now I hold the cards, and I'm not gambling.

About the Author

Angie began putting her feelings on paper at a young age. She found writing was her way of dealing with problems, as well as communicating more successfully with the people she cared about most. She is a mother of 3, a wife, an English teacher, and a firm believer that putting pen to paper and releasing your thoughts can free you!

Made in the USA
Monee, IL
27 June 2022